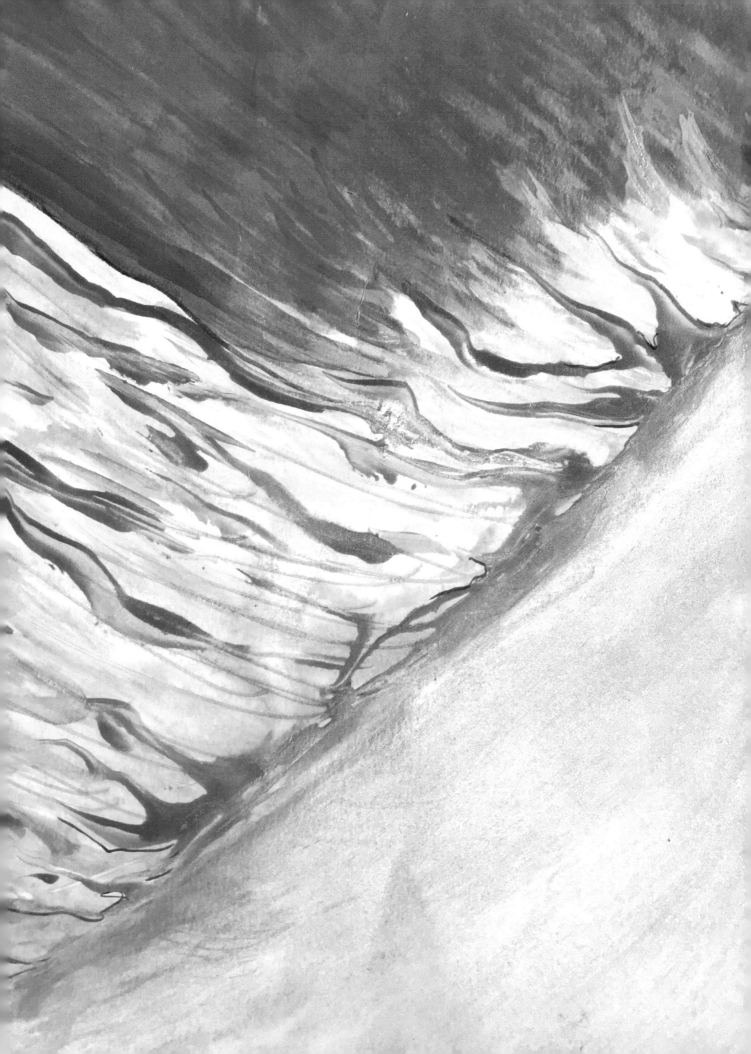

For Tai Nakoa and Bing Kree Manu

2nd Edition 2019
Illustrations copyright © 2018 by Ezban Brownlee

Identifiers: LCCN: **2018908363**
ISBN **978-0-9978738-2-5** *(Hardcover)*
ISBN **978-0-9978738-6-3** *(Paperback)*

The text of this book is set in Tempus Sans
The illustrations were created using watercolor & acrylic

GreyHouse Press

THE CRYPTID CARNIVAL

by ROSALIE BARDO

illustrations by Ezban Brownlee

Deep in the
woods on a
magical night,

A young boy
fell upon
a wondrous sight!

"The night
for
dragons,
dreamers,
and all
make-
believers!

Don't be afraid, no need to run.
Step inside and join the fun!"

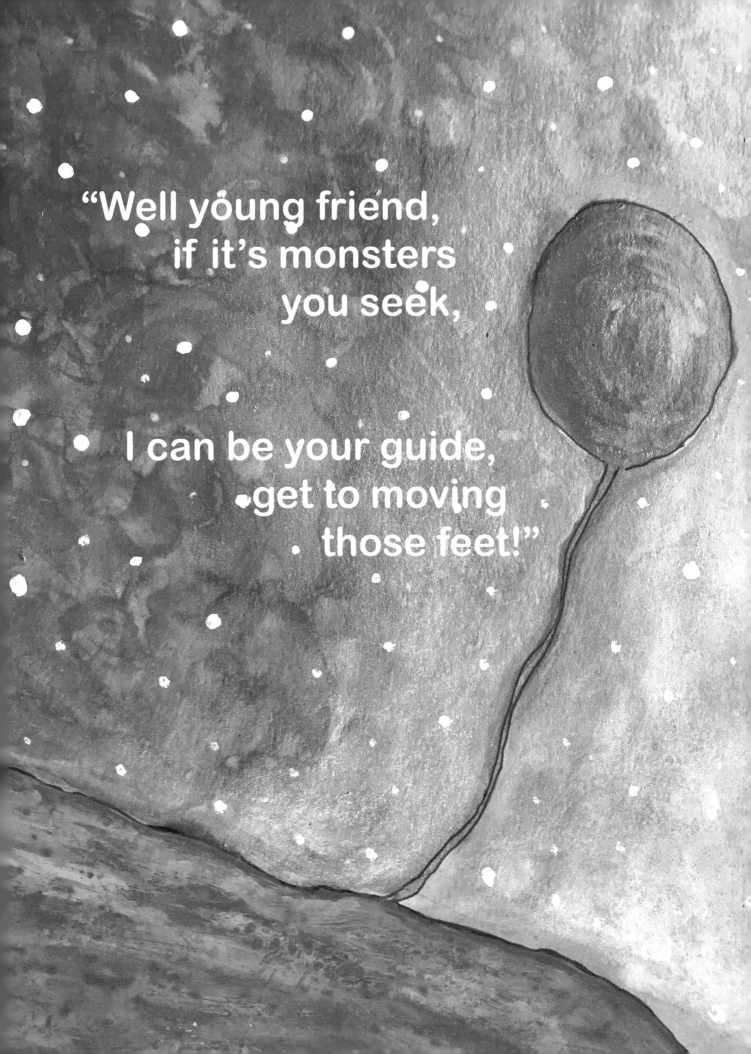

"First stop here,
on our marvelous route,
is Le Dwarf Diner of Gandermount."

"Now we've entered
the Cave of Wonder!"

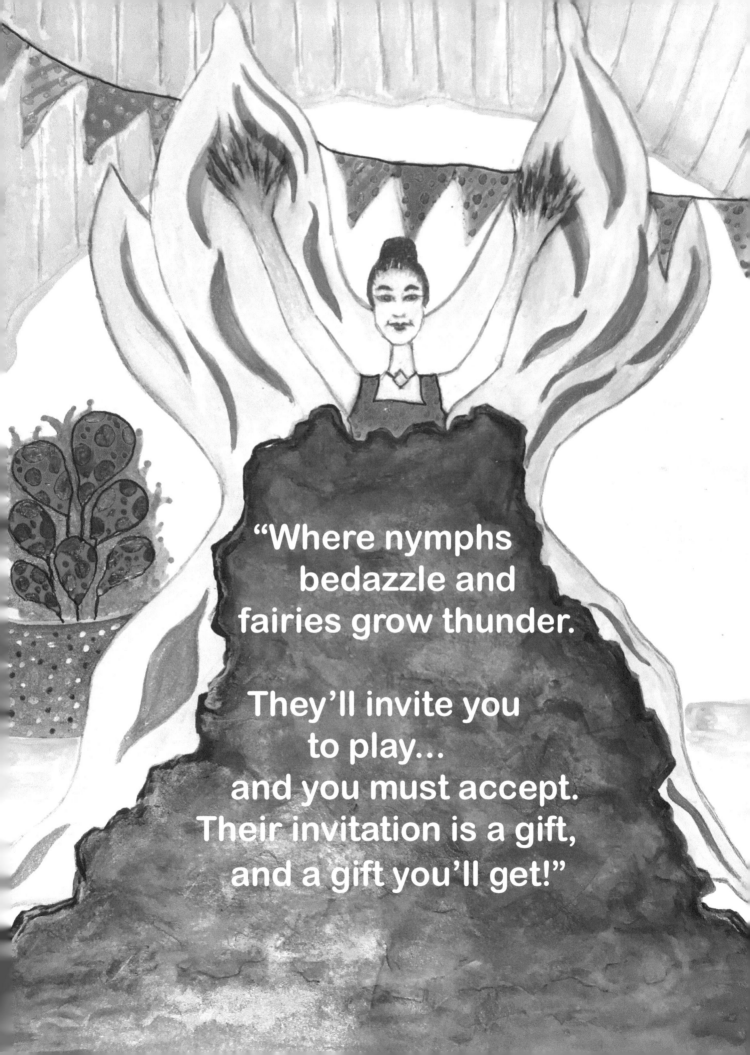

"Come my friend,
there's much
left to see!

Time to ride
the Thunderbird
and greet
the Yeti!"

"No worries my friend,
    the Yeti won't judge.

No size, color, or smell
    will keep them from us."

"My Thunderbird,
humor me, but
please fly low.

We don't
want to miss the
Chupacabra
dance below."

The
Lake
Eerie
monster,
known
to most as Bessie."

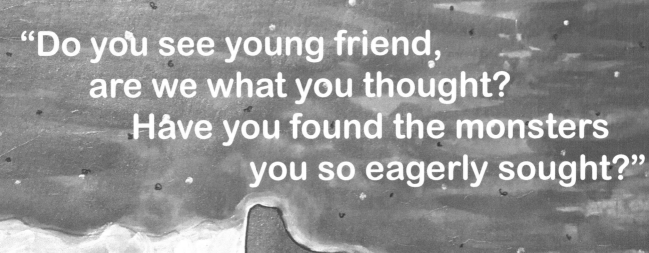

"We are thinkers, creators, a magical sort.
No hoaxes on this ride, no words to contort

"But dear boy;
don't you see,
there is nothing
to fix.

You are what you are,
and we're all
meant to mix.

Imagine how boring
this life would be,
if we never embraced
our unique qualities!"

"We can all live together in peace and unity, if I accept you and you accept me.

You're right
mister,
I agree.
Let's be
the
best of
friends
that friends
can be!

YOU ARE WORTHY OF
ALL GOOD THINGS.